For Mum and Dad –
thanks for your support

and encouragement

PUFFIN BOOKS

Published by the Penguin Group
Penguin Books Ltd, 80 Strand, London WC2R 0RL, England
Penguin Putnam Inc., 375 Hudson Street, New York, New York 10014, USA
Penguin Books Australia Ltd, 250 Camberwell Road, Camberwell, Victoria 3124, Australia
Penguin Books Canada Ltd, 10 Alcorn Avenue, Toronto, Ontario, Canada M4V 3B2
Penguin Books India (P) Ltd, 11 Community Centre, Panchsheel Park, New Delhi – 110 017, India
Penguin Books (NZ) Ltd, Cnr Rosedale and Airborne Roads, Albany, Auckland, New Zealand
Penguin Books (South Africa) (Pty) Ltd, 24 Sturdee Avenue, Rosebank 2196, South Africa

Penguin Books Ltd, Registered Offices: 80 Strand, London WC2R 0RL, England

www.penguin.com

First published 2002
1 3 5 7 9 10 8 6 4 2

Set in Fink

Printed in China by Midas Printing International Ltd

British Library Cataloguing in Publication Data
A CIP catalogue record for this book is available from the British Library

ISBN 0–140–56859–X

Toby's Funfair Fish

Nathan Reed

PUFFIN BOOKS

Toby loved going to the fair.
He'd been waiting all week and
now, at last, it was time.

First, he **whizzed** down the helter skelter.

Next, he ZOOMED around on the dodgems.

After that, he took off
on his favourite flying ride.

Toby was high up in the sky when he spotted...

goldfish!

Toby only needed to
catch one duck to win a fish.
He reached forward very slowly
and very carefully.

"Yes!"
he squealed.
"I've done it!"
Toby chose the only stripy fish.

"I'm going to call you Moby,"
said Toby. "Let's go home."

Toby found a **huge** glass bowl for his new pet.

Perfect! he thought.
But the little fish didn't look very happy.

So Toby tried to cheer him up.

He did handstands.

And juggled his toys.

He did star jumps.

He even sang songs.

But Moby still looked sad.

"How can I make you happy, Moby?"
Toby asked through the glass bowl.
He was getting tired and didn't
know what to do next.

If I had a **dogfish**, thought Toby,

I would take him for walks.

If I had a **clownfish**, thought Toby,

we could tell jokes and make up tricks!

But he might play a trick on me!

If I had a **moonfish**, thought Toby,
I would visit her in my rocket.

But I might hit a shooting star!

If I had a **piranha** fish, thought Toby,

I would feed him all my favourite things.

But he might want to eat me!

Suddenly Toby jumped up.
"Yes! I know how to make Moby smile!"
he cried.

So Toby began to ...

draw

paint

stick

cut

until at last ...

...Toby showed Moby his very own special fairground.

Moby flipped his tail and **smiled**.

His bowl now felt just like home.

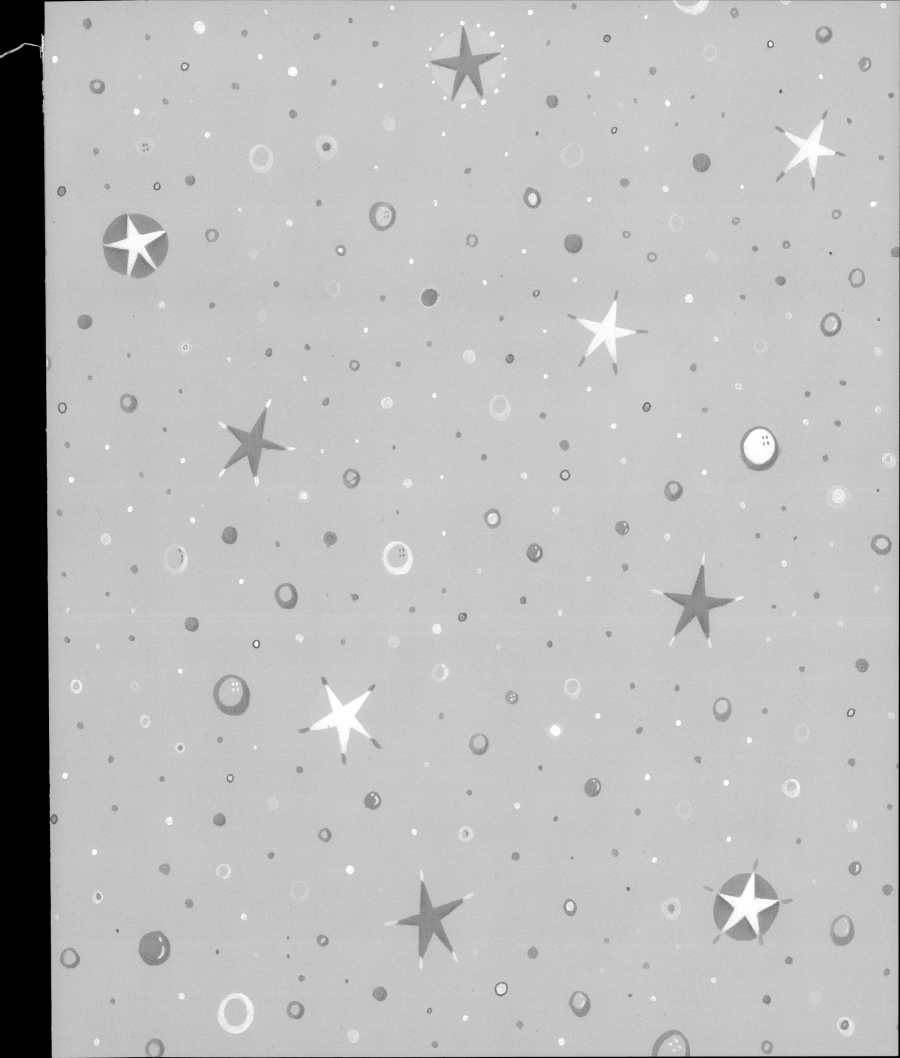